*B*laze atop *S*wallow Hill Lookout

a Firehawks romance story
by
M. L. Buchman

Buchman Bookworks

1

The "airshow" was spectacular, from a
distance. Marta Chavez scanned the horizon
every fifteen minutes like a responsible fire
lookout. But she spent the rest of her time
watching the firefight over at Gray Wolf
Summit, about twenty miles to the northeast
of her tower. They were deep in the Lolo
wilderness, rougher than Colorado, and
only Alaska was more wild.

First the smokies had spilled out of the
sky, their parachutes blooming and dancing
about in the fire-driven winds. Then the
new four-jet BAe 146 tanker had arrived

on the fire, dropping great swaths of dark red retardant. A half dozen helos zipped through the air: a trio of the big converted Black Hawk helicopters called Firehawks that were at least as impressive as the BAe 146, and a second trio of little MD500s that flitted about the sky.

She always loved watching the MD500s. They only carried a little water, a hundred and thirty gallons versus the thousand of the Firehawk or the three thousand dropped by the BAe, but they could slip right up to a spot fire, blast it out of existence, and dance out of the way with a tight pirouette. It always reminded her of her childhood dreams of being a ballerina, dashed by the advent of breasts at the age of thirteen. Ballerinas were supposed to be willowy— even better if you were short and willowy.

Marta was tall and had ended up… very not willowy. Her mama had always said it was God's will; personally, Marta felt gypped.

So she'd gone out for track instead and that had led to cross-country, which was nuts for a woman with curves, but a doubled-up sports bra had cured the worst of that—still her chest hurt like the Madonna after some of the bigger runs.

Ultimately, running along the forest trails and logging roads of Coeur d'Alene, Idaho had led to a summer job as a fire lookout. Now she could watch helicopters dance so lightly on the winds that they reminded her that she wasn't so graceful. But still she couldn't stop watching them; her arms ached from holding the binoculars aloft even though her elbows were propped on the edge of her cabin's table.

It was the eighth fire she'd found already this summer, which earned her the dubious honor of being the number one spotter this season. She was just glad that none of them had been anywhere near her. The airshow must have really rattled Gray Wolf's cage as this fire burned right at the base of his lookout tower's mountain; which explained why she'd spotted it first—he'd had no view straight down off his cliff. They had it contained now; ground crews would be in to kill it in the morning. He'd never been threatened, but it could have gone bad.

Marta scanned the thickly-clad conifer mountains of the Lolo National Forest. Her first year she'd thought of it in mountains: Goat, White, Cougar. Now in her second season she knew it by the dark slashes of recent fires or the bright green of new growth after last season's: Colgate, Crazy Creek, Loco, and all the rest.

She finished the round, her last of the day, and called it in, "Swallow Hill calling, no fires except Wolf's Den. Out of service."

"Roger that, Swallow Hill. Well done today." She liked Vic, the U.S. Forest Service ranger in charge of this sector. He always had something nice to say. She'd carried quite a fantasy about him during the first season…until she'd found out he was forty with a gut and married. But he had one of those deep, smooth voices.

Just like Helo 41. She could listen to Tyler Walker, 41's lone pilot, report vectors and drops of his MD500 all day—he had a liquid Colorado accent, overly polite with just the sweetest hint of cowboy. But quite why a girl from Coeur d'Alene would swoon over such a thing—she'd never even been to Colorado. Didn't even know what he looked like, but she did enjoy listening to that voice of his.

Even though the official day of 9 a.m. to 6 p.m. was over for the lookouts, she kept both her radio and her scanner on as she made dinner. On the radio she heard Gray Wolf still working the communications with the ground crew. In the deep canyons of the Lolo, it was common that one ground crew couldn't talk to another, so the lookout tower would act as a relay.

She took her water jug down to the cistern and filled it up. The rainwater off her lookout tower roof had been collected throughout the winter into a concrete cistern built beneath her lookout tower on Swallow Hill. Hill—that just wasn't right. Swallow Hill might not be one of the big peaks—Cougar ruled the area up at almost nine thousand feet—but at seventy-five hundred, her "Hill" should have been respected as a mountain. She often felt sorry for it.

"We'll show 'em, girl," she patted the rock at the base of the steps before climbing back up toward the lookout's cabin.

The lookout tower itself was new, as far as lookout towers went. Most had been built by the Depression-era crews almost a century ago. Swallow Hill had been burned over in the sixties and had to be replaced. Rather than the elegance of one of the CCC's massive wooden structures, her tower was five stories of steel lattice. It had been built tall so that the view would be clear when the timber regrew. Fifty years after the burnover and the tallest trees were still only a dozen feet high. Most of the upper slope was lush alpine meadow. It gave her an amazing view from her twelve-foot square cab at the top.

A hundred and forty-four square feet of pure functionality. A two-foot wide "deck" wrapped all of the way around so that she could open and close the big shutters at the beginning and end of the season, and could clean the wrap-around glass windows in between.

Everything in its place, because if it wasn't, she'd trip on it. Dad's fifth-wheel camper was bigger than this place, and that was before he opened the slide-outs. The cab's center was dominated by the two-foot diameter disk of the Osborne Fire Finder to let her pinpoint a blaze. Around the perimeter was a chair, a cot, and a strip of counter that was desk, workbench, and kitchen. The cooler sat underneath the counter along with her pack and all of her dry groceries. Finding a spot for both her running shoes and her boots had been a problem until she'd decided to always keep one or the other on while she was awake.

She liked the contrast to her own room in her parents' home. She was only in Coeur d'Alene for the month between the fire and ski seasons, plus two days off every other week. But it was her childhood room. A dense clutter of kid projects, high school trophies, and a ton of crap she always meant to shed but could never quite bring herself to do, crowded the room impossibly. The only way to make her bed at home was to be on it.

Here she was neat as a pin; a different person. Here she wasn't six inches taller than any of her siblings. Here every guy on the block didn't know her, cat calling

every time she went out for a run. Swallow
Hill Lookout was just the watching and
the silence. A golden eagle circled high on
the wind above the cab; silent and shining
in the low sunlight. A swallow swooped
busily in and out of the swallow box she'd
packed in this spring and attached to the
steel trestle. It was ridiculous to have no
swallows on Swallow Hill, and they hadn't
nested among the sparse trees last season.

She'd been very cheered when the pair of
swallows had claimed the box and begun nest
building in it. The first tiny cheep sounding
from the box's small round hole had been
an almost transcendental experience. She'd
rushed up and down the five-story trestle
between every fifteen minute scan of the
horizon...and barely been able to walk the
next day her legs were so sore.

The young had only fledged yesterday,
making the terrifyingly heroic flight from
bird box to the opposite side of the trestle,
and then back to the bird box. By evening
parents and children were soaring wild loops
around the lookout tower clearing the air of
any bugs foolish enough to brave the cool

evening. The golden eagle had surveyed the quick and tiny swallows, as well as Marta herself, carefully. Apparently deciding that neither of them would make a tasty meal, she'd soared off seeking lusher pickings.

Marta waved at the flitting swallows then ducked into the cab and began boiling the water on her small gas stove. She was a third-generation Idahoan of Mexican descent with a taste for Italian food that she cultivated at her uncle's knee; Mama's much younger brother was often more her big brother than the two that Mama had provided her with. That was before Uncle Manuel had moved to Seattle to become a big time chef with an elegantly slender Italian wife. Graziella's problem was that she was so nice that Marta couldn't even hold being willowy against her. They'd become like sisters—which Marta had always wanted—both were dusky skinned… and that was the only part of their features that were in common.

While the water boiled, which took a while at this altitude, she flicked on the radio scanner, and began chopping sun-dried tomatoes and olives. The scanner gave her the bigger picture of what was happening in the area. Her radio was tuned only to the primary Forest Service frequency, but a lot went on among the heights of the Lolo National Forest and the Bitterroot-Selway Wilderness.

Last summer Tess Weaver and Jack Parker had done a whole courtship thing on a higher frequency. It had started out as radio chess, something that Marta was good enough at that she could generally follow their games without a board. When their conversations had shifted to more personal matters, she'd tuned off their frequency to give them a little privacy.

This season it was Tom up on Gray Wolf and some wildlife biologist following wolves. The discussions about wolves had been fascinating, but then they too had gotten all mushy and personal, and she'd taken to skipping their "private" frequency. Because of that she'd missed most of a rather dangerous rescue this afternoon when they'd had to use a helicopter to short-haul the biologist to safety.

There was no privacy on mountain radio, but each lookout extended the courtesy of pretending not to listen. Otherwise it became a very long and lonely season. Marta often traded recipes with Angeline up on Old Crag and with Jack on Cougar because Tess couldn't cook soup.

Marta tossed in the pasta, then diced in what she could salvage of her carrots and rather sad small zucchini. It was getting close to her bi-weekly resupply trip off the mountain and, with no refrigeration, veggies were scarce at the moment.

The airwaves were quiet tonight, except for the last of the airshow still going on around Gray Wolf Summit. They were down to the Incident Air Commander flying an airplane well above the fire for a good view and the big Firehawks laying down the main strikes. Tyler ducked his MD500 in and out of the fray with smooth precision.

She always waited for those moments. He never replied to a drop command with a simple, "Roger." That would be too impolite for his breeding and his sense of humor.

"That little ol' spot? Why it's hardly a fire a-tall. You sure I should be snuffing her out? If I do, she'll never grow up all tall and proper like."

She could feel the ICA rolling his eyes somewhere far above. "Just hit the damn thing, Tyler."

"Yes sir. Your order is this flyboy's command. Just checking was all." And then he'd hammer it with perfect precision and turn back for the next load of water or retardant.

With her luck, he probably looked like a toad. Not that she'd ever meet him. Still, didn't hurt a girl to dream a little bit.

She served up her bowl of pasta and blanched veggies, sprinkled on the olives and sun-dried tomatoes, drizzling it with the oil from the tomatoes, and shaved the last of her precious Parmigiano-Reggiano cheese on it. She raised a small glass of red wine to the west in a salute to her uncle and the fair Graziella. It was just box wine, but it was the best she could offer—glass bottles weighed far too much to pack in both directions as Swallow Hill Lookout was six steep miles beyond the closest parking spot.

2

"No, Mom. I like my job," Marta growled
at the first squirrel to peek around a young
spruce tree to see who was starting up the
long trail to the peak of Swallow Hill.

"I like my winter job too," she told an
overly curious robin. Ski season she worked
at the Silver Mountain Resort as a waitress.
"Free lift tickets and next season they'll let
me try out for ski patrol." Which would pay
worse due to lack of tips, but irritate her
much less.

"I know it's not Schweitzer, Mama" the
premier resort of Northern Idaho.

The robin flew off deciding that she didn't want anything to do with this half-mad lunatic. It happened to Marta every time she came off the mountain during the season. She reverted into some form of her normal self that she wasn't real happy with. And Mama had been on a roll because "that Janson girl just married your old flame the Malcolm boy."

"She's welcome to him," Marta told a garter snake, a big one almost two feet long. It scowled at her from its sunny rock where the trail turned to avoid an old slide that had taken down several alders and a six-inch maple. The alders, typically were doing well, the maple was turning back into mulch. The "Malcolm boy" had been good enough in bed, an event she had made sure Mama never knew about, but about as mentally exciting as watching paint dry, which fit for a housepainter. Of course "that Janson girl" hadn't been the brightest color in the palette either, so maybe it worked for her.

"I know I won't meet a man on the tops of mountains," she shouted at the snake when he flicked out a long red and black-tipped tongue at her. As she was neither a predator nor rational, he returned to enjoying his sun-warmed rock.

It was a problem, but it wasn't one she was terribly worried about. No one came up Swallow Hill. If she had five visitors a summer it was a big deal. And the guys she met waitressing at the ski resort up on Silver Mountain, well, even she wasn't that kind of desperate. Maybe if she worked her way up to Schweitzer or Sun Valley, but those were coveted spots on the ski patrol circuit and, worse, she'd bet the men-type opportunities weren't any more fruitful in those places even if by all rights they should be.

"But, Marta-*cara*, we worry about you soooo much!" Marta mimicked Mama's voice to a turkey vulture that carved the air at the first vista lookout, an hour up the trail.

Since when had her Mexican family become so Italian?

Again Uncle Manuel's fault. She'd been raised in a lingual hash of Mexican, Italian, and English. No wonder nobody understood her when she got angry—other than her own family, of course.

At the halfway point up the trail, she needed a break and dropped the heavy pack loaded with her next two weeks of supplies. She heard the bright *tink* and cursed. At the very bottom of her pack she'd tucked two jars of the spaghetti sauce that she and Mama had put up last fall. Still not really understanding Marta's isolation, Mama had insisted that Marta should have something homemade to serve if a nice man came by. The glass had broken against a rock when she'd unthinkingly dropped her pack. There was no point in digging the mess out now. She'd been right, glass was too heavy, but she'd been in such a hurry to get out of the house that she hadn't taken the time to empty the jars into baggies.

By the time she reached the summit, she had chaffed shoulders, a sore back, and the bottom corner of her pack and the right hip of her shorts were both stained tomato red.

3

Detrick met her at the bottom of the lookout stairs with his pack already on. He headed down the mountain with barely a, "No fires. See you in twelve days." He was hustling down to be with his new girlfriend, whom she wished luck. Dating a lookout substitute meant that you saw him only briefly every three days, because the rest of the summer he was cycling up and down to various towers.

He wasn't her type anyway. He reminded her of all of the jocks who used to try and grope her in school. He seemed nice enough in the moments they traded places, and didn't stare at her chest—too much. He also left the cab as neat as he found it, which she appreciated but he never slowed down enough for her to thank him.

She did her first scan to confirm Detrick's assessment and then unloaded her pack. At least only one jar was broken.

Then she felt an itch.

It was the itch that her Uncle Manuel had tried to teach her, "It is when what is missing is too subtle. You can no longer taste that you need more thyme or oregano, but you know that the balance, it isn't right. Then you must become very careful. A mistake now and the whole sauce must go down the drain. But still the sauce is incomplete and must be finished. Slow down and listen. You will feel an itch, a tiny push from some part of you that knows about food and flavors. What it tells you, that will be the right answer."

She felt one of those.

Marta slowed down, waited, putting everything away. Produce in the cooler, dry goods and cans on the shelves. Two new books, one only a little stained with red sauce, on the tiny shelf above her desk.

Out of the soggy shorts and into clean ones.

Then, rather than standing at the Osborne Fire Finder, she stepped out onto the narrow porch with her binoculars. She started the circuit at Gray Wolf Summit to the northeast because it was one of the clearest landmarks in the area. From the burn at the base of the summit, she swept slow arcs; first along the horizon, then lower and lower until she was looking down the cliff of Swallow Hill's north and east face.

Then she moved to the north side of the tower and did the same thing. She always went around it "contrariwise." Her dad said that she did everything backwards because she was left-handed. What had been an idle joke had turned into an act of defiance and finally a force of habit. She'd learned that doing things "contrariwise" let her see things that she wouldn't otherwise if she was being "normal."

She was around to the south side of Swallow Hill when she spotted the faint puff of smoke. It disappeared almost the instant that she saw it, because young fires could do that.

She didn't move the binoculars from that point for three long minutes.

The breeze was a light brush out of the south as well. And it carried…wood smoke.

Another puff and she had it pinpointed. Not taking her eyes off the spot, she fumbled around until she found the doorway into the cab. She spun the Osborne into position and looked through the two brass sights just as the smoke went from puffy white to steady gray.

She pulled the radio off her hip. "Gray Wolf, this is Swallow Hill. I need a cross approximately two miles south of my tower."

Tom up on Gray Wolf came back moments later, "Two-three-nine degrees."

"Roger that," Marta plotted the cross quickly, double-checked everything, then called Vic. "Fire control, this is Swallow Hill. Confirming new fire due south of my tower at…" she read out the longitude and latitude. "Just gone steady. No eyes on the blaze, but estimate one acre based on plume."

"Catching them earlier and earlier, Marta. You know this blaze puts you ahead of the all-time record: number of fires spotted by an individual this far through the season. Ten more and you'll break the all-time season record."

"Oh joy," she radioed back.

Vic's laugh made her feel worlds better. "I have a chopper heading your way. He's in the area, we'll get some eyes on the prize before we call the troops."

4

Marta ducked and cursed as the small helo buzzed her tower from behind. She'd been out on the south deck again, and hadn't heard him coming from the opposite side of the tower.

Helo 41 slewed to a halt, hovering, and turned so that the pilot was facing her from just a hundred feet away. The sun was behind him and she could only see the shadows of the man at the controls.

"Afternoon, Ms. Swallow Hill." Tyler. She did her best to avoid a girly sigh…and really wished she could see him better.

She pulled her radio off her belt and keyed the Transmit button. "Afternoon yourself, Master Tyler."

"I hear you found another one for us to play with."

She pointed down the slope toward the gray puff that was already going black with soot.

Helo 41 twisted to the left and she could see the silhouette of the pilot looking down and to the side, but still couldn't tell his age or build. "Yep, that does indeed look like you have a fire, Ms. Swallow Hill. And right on your front stoop."

Then the helicopter twisted back to face her rather than diving down for a closer look.

"If you don't mind my sayin', Ms. Swallow Hill. Never have seen you out of your glass tower before. I can see that I was missing a fine sight. A fine sight indeed."

Before she could think how to respond, he'd slammed over his controls and half rolled into a plummet down the valley.

So, he liked the way she looked. Big deal. Most guys liked how she looked. Then she raised her binoculars and focused them down the slope again.

"Wish't," she imitated his voice, "I'd a thought to be lookin' through this here contraption when you were a might closer, Mister Tyler." Instead of Tyler's smooth Colorado, it came out more Mexican-Italian-Texan which sounded even stupider out loud than she'd imagined. A burst of giggles tickled its way up her throat and she was never one to hold back a giggle when it came.

So, he thought she was pretty? Well, with that gorgeous voice of his, he didn't have to be a handsome one. Maybe she'd find a way to meet him…when there wasn't a fire on her mountain.

For now she'd just sit and watch the airshow.

5

Six hours later she *wished* she could just sit and watch.

Tankers were on other fires. Helos were spread thin. Most of the smokies were in Colorado. And the Swallow Creek Fire was taking unfair advantage of their lack of attention. The south side of Swallow Hill was engulfed in flame and the plume of smoke kept blanking out Marta's view.

She'd retreated into the cab, closed the windows and doors, and donned a dust filter mask so that she didn't choke on the ash.

"Hang on, sweet thing," was all the warning she had before Tyler unleashed a hundred and forty gallons of water over her cab. It whumped down onto the roof with a crash like thunder. The half-ton of water striking in a single blow made the cab shake its head like a wet dog shedding bathwater. The structure shuddered and then calmed.

It was a good move, once she was over the shock of it. Soak down the tower so that no stray ember alighted and caught the place on fire.

Soaking down the tower.

That was definitely not a good sign. You didn't do that unless the fire was close.

If she had to move, it was going to be fast. Her big pack would slow her down too much. She grabbed her fanny pack and shoved in a small medical kit along with spare batteries for her radio, and a water bottle. She pulled down her favorite family photo, parents and two hopelessly dense but terribly handsome older brothers gathered at Manuel and Graziella's wedding. She kissed the photo for good luck, snapped a can of bear-repellant pepper spray onto the belt along with a foil fire shelter—because a firefighter is always prepared, even when she's a lookout tower woman on the verge of totally freaking out.

And then she couldn't think what else to do.

The helos were losing the battle and she was losing options.

Ten minutes. She was a fast runner. Marta would give them ten more minutes and then she'd be jackrabbitting down the trail and to hell with the firefight.

6

At fifteen minutes, she'd eased down three of the five flights of steps, reluctant to leave the Swallow Hill Lookout un-womaned in the middle of a fire.

The air was thick with smoke and growing hotter by the minute. She could taste the char right through her filter mask. The fire's roar, always a distant thunder in her experience, was now a passing freight train. It wouldn't be long before it was a jet engine at max thrust, and just as hot.

At seventeen minutes, she'd made it down another flight and the steel handrail was warm against her palm. The air was hot and her breath was coming too fast.

Was the air clearer? Or was it her imagination? She looked up and couldn't see the cab at all. It was wrapped in a shroud of smoke that was climbing the hill and soaring aloft.

Okay. It was her imagination. That and she was getting closer to the ground.

The airshow had become a distant sound, muffled by the fire's thunder, but she could still pick them out. Another helo had just arrived. A tanker as well. But Tyler had left to refuel just a moment ago.

She checked her watch, had to rub at her eyes to make them focus.

Duh!

Marta rinsed her eyes from the water bottle, dried them with the hem of her t-shirt, and then pulled on the goggles that habit had shoved onto her hair.

Now she could see her watch. Tyler had been gone twenty minutes. Long enough to refuel in Missoula and get back here? Probably. Maybe he was the returning helicopter she could hear circling above the tower. That meant there was still only him and the tanker. It made her feel safer, knowing he was close by.

She heard him setting up for another pass, then she heard a high buzzing sound—impossibly close to her. She thought she saw motion out of the corner of her eye, but it was gone into the smoke too fast to be sure.

Seconds later she heard an odd crunch. Something mechanical and it didn't sound good.

"Goddamn it!" Tyler. On the radio. Swearing. That didn't sound good at all.

"Helo 41 report!" The Incident Air Commander called down when Tyler didn't continue.

"Hobbyist drone over the fire. It came up out of the smoke and I think I hit it."

"Any issue?"

"Assessing."

Marta tried to breathe. Tried to count seconds in her head. Tried to think of some way to help him—

"Mayday! Mayday! Mayday! This is Helo 41. Tail rotor not responding, I have to put it down, fast. Visibility zero. Mayday! Mayday! Mayday!"

"Tyler!" Marta screamed at the sky.

And then, almost as if he'd heard her, his helo plunged down out of the smoke so close by that it felt as if she could touch him.

A blade clipped the steel tower not five feet above her head. With a horrible metallic rending sound and a high whistle, a chunk of rotor blade flashed by her head.

She dove down the last flight of stairs, rolled on the ground, and looked up in time to see the helicopter hit the rocky slope, bounce upward, then thump down hard, crushing one of its long skids.

He'd been moving so fast; the helicopter careened and tumbled down the slope.

Marta was away from the platform and racing after the helo even while it still rolled. The five thin blades battered and flailed at the rock. Chunks flew in every direction.

A hard dodge to one side and a four-foot section missed her by mere inches. She barely noticed, her whole being focused on reaching Tyler through the mayhem.

The helo balanced upside down for a long moment, perched on the remains of its rotor head. Then in an almost lazy last gasp, it rolled back onto the meadow—most of the way onto its belly.

Marta reached the bird and finally realized where it had stopped. Another half roll and it would have tumbled right off of Swallow Hill, a two thousand foot fall down a cliff face too steep to walk without a rope.

She reached the door, yanking with sheer adrenaline until she had it free.

Someone was shouting on the radio.

Wasn't Tyler.

So didn't matter.

Tyler lay sideways in his harness. Slowly, so slowly, he twisted around to look at her.

He had a half dozen cuts on his face and was bleeding from several of them, but none of them badly. Despite the cuts and blood, she could see that while he wasn't beautiful—so much for girlish fantasies—his face had a ruggedness that was quite attractive.

He offered her a sideways smile, then hissed and reached up a hand to gently test a split lip. His eyes had not left her face for a second.

"Hello there, Ms. Swallow Hill. Sorry for dropping in unannounced like this. Poor form for a gentleman come calling."

"Terribly poor form," she did her best to match his tone. "Let's get y'all out of there before something worse happens."

"There's only one of me."

"What?" She climbed into the cockpit to help him.

"Y'all isn't singular, Ms. Hill. It's for a group of folks. Especially if they're from the Deep South, which I'm not."

"Then how's that sentence supposed to go," she worked his harness free and did her best to ignore how close together they were in the tiny space, she kneeling on the tilted co-pilot's seat, him still strapped into the pilot's position.

"Should be: 'Let's get you out of there…'." He spoke in a deadpan accentless voice, clearly making fun of her, but trailed off in a way she didn't like.

There were no obvious signs of blood. So maybe he'd just been concussed rather than collapsing into shock. She'd taken the standard First Aid course for lookouts, but it wasn't much. The bottom line for a lookout was: do anything to yourself worse than a small cut and you're screwed. Help was a long way off.

Between them, they maneuvered him out of the cockpit. The smoke was getting thicker and she'd lost her mask and goggles somewhere during the sprint. A path of destruction had been flattened through the tall meadow grass by the helicopter's tumble. It was a wonder he was still alive.

"My ankle isn't working quite right."

They both looked down as he clung to her. It was twisted to the side. Grotesquely.

She looked at him, liking that he was a couple inches taller than her own height, and did her best to keep her voice light, "I don't think it's supposed to look like that."

"Not if I want to go walking anywhere on it," he agreed and continued to hang onto her.

"Where's my pilot? Tyler, report!" The ICA's voice screamed from her radio.

She pulled it out.

"I've got him. But his ankle is broken. Request immediate medivac."

The stream of vitriol that poured out of the radio was quite impressive.

"You'll have to forgive him. He's rarely a passionate man, except about his pilots," Tyler whispered close to her jaw, with his nose practically buried in her ear. "Hey, Ms. Swallow. You smell right nice. Like—"

Something romantic?

"Like, tomato sauce."

Crap! She must have rubbed her hand in her hair while she was cleaning up her mess from the hike up. "It's an…old family recipe."

"Good enough to eat."

She considered taking offense, but if he was coming onto her, he wasn't doing it with a grope or a grab, so she'd tolerate it for the moment.

"Swallow Hill, this is ICA. I can't get to you. The entire peak is shrouded in smoke and you have my only helo in the area. Can you confirm the hobbyist drone?"

Tyler pointed with the hand that wasn't around her shoulder at the mangled tail of his wrecked aircraft. There was the remains of something white and mechanical caught in the rear rotor blade. She didn't know how to fly, but she knew a helicopter didn't do so well without its rear rotor.

"Roger that, ICA. Have visual on a hobbyist drone, or at least the remains of one."

"I'm gonna kill the bugger that flew that thing. I swear I am. Tyler, I have to pull back the tanker; I can't have him hitting a second drone. We can't get through the smoke even if I had a helo local. You'll have to take care of yourself."

Marta held the mike up to Tyler's mouth and hit the Transmit key for him.

"Not a problem, Mark. I'm downright comfortable where I'm standing." And Marta was too. Very comfortable. He had an arm around her shoulders, and she around his waist, as if it was the most natural thing in the world for them to stand that way. He was just an inch or so taller than she was and she was upgrading that ruggedness to very good-looking.

"No," the ICA called back. "You're not. The fire is going to crest the ridge in ten minutes and there isn't a thing we can do to stop it, even if there weren't any other drones in the air and I had the full fleet. Swallow Hill, you keep my pilot alive, god damn it."

Though there was nothing to see, Marta became aware of the sounds for the first time since the crash.

She heard the heavy roar of the BAe 146 jet climbing clear of the area. High above, she heard the strong buzz of the ICA's twin-engine airplane circling thousands of feet above the fire.

Close to hand, there was a deep, basso roar that shook the air. So loud now that it felt as if it was shaking the ground.

"A FEAR fire," Tyler whispered, and this time she didn't feel any tease close beside her ear.

It was the worst stage of a wildfire before it overran you, the Fuck Everything And Run moment.

7

"Ten minutes," **Tyler sounded** perfectly calm. Dangerously so.

Marta remembered a cross-country race. She and a top runner from Boise had been deep in the woods and way ahead of the pack. They'd run against each other before and Barb was a tough contender.

Then Barb had caught a foot on a high tree root and crashed to the ground. And she'd just sat there. Cheerful. Glad to chat and answer questions. But she hadn't had a single thought for the race. No complaints while Marta had checked both her ankles which appeared fine. Barb hadn't had any reaction even when she looked down at her broken wrist bent over backward. So decisive just a moment before, she appeared perfectly calm once injured.

Shock.

Tyler was in shock which meant it was up to her.

Hightailing it down the trail was no longer an option. She should have left twenty minutes ago; she checked her watch. Thirty minutes ago.

But at some moment very soon, Tyler was going to start feeling his broken ankle.

The cab wouldn't do them any good, even if they could get up to it. And the shattered helo was no option at all.

"Tyler," she cupped his chin and turned him to look at her. "Hang onto the helo, I have to check something out."

He grumbled about trading soft-and-warm for hard-and-metal, but made the shift.

Marta crawled back into the cockpit and looked around, but couldn't see it. It had to be here somewhere. She stuck her head back out.

"Where's your emergency shelter?" The foil shelters were the tool of last resort and she knew the pilots had to fly with one.

"In the door pocket, pilot's side," he said it with enough clarity that she wondered if he really was in shock, or if he was just keeping a humorous façade up against the pain.

She looked back down into the tiny cabin. There was no pilot's door, there was only granite and tufts of grass where it should be. Crawling back out of the cabin, she looked around, still no sign of it, though there was the debris trail that started near the tower and was scattered across a hundred yards of the slope, she didn't see anything as large as a door.

The debris field continued past the helicopter and…

She moved as close as she dared to the edge of the cliff and looked down through the thickening smoke. Fifty yards below them there might have been a piece of helicopter big enough to be a door, but it was far out of their reach.

She had the one shelter on her belt. But as tempting as the idea of sharing a fire shelter with Tyler might be, it wouldn't work. The shelter was designed to provide close protection for a single person. Maybe if they were both petite…but they weren't.

"Story of my life," she mumbled as she looked around the barren hilltop for other options.

8

Her final glimpse before shutting the lid was of thick black clouds of smoke colored with the deep orange of fast-approaching flame.

"And I had so hoped, Ms. Swallow Hill, that my first water adventure with you might include something like skinny dipping. Seems my imagining came close. Care to complete a man's wildest dreams, Ms. Hill?" She could hear his gentle smile even if she couldn't see it in the pitch black.

Marta appreciated it all the more because there hadn't been time to move Tyler gently. The sweat of pain poured off him, but he'd kept his tone light and friendly despite the anguish of getting him in here. Whether the effort or the terror had done it, he was shaking off the shock. At least for the moment.

They were submerged up to their necks in the concrete cistern of her lookout tower's drinking water. The heavy steel lid above them was closed, for whatever protection it might afford. Then, draped like an air bubble over their heads, she'd spread her fire shelter. It was the only chance they had. *Santa Maria Madre di Dios.* Childhood prayers weren't helping her much. She focused back on Tyler, except she couldn't see him in the dark.

"How about a rain check on the skinny dipping?" She barely managed the thought around her raw nerves. Now that she had done everything she could other than wait, the impact of their precarious position was striking home.

"Rain, might help some. Douse this fire down a bit," it helped that his tone had finally taken on an anxious note. His voice was becoming clearer, recovering from his shock. Sharing her fear with someone else made the situation a bit more bearable. A very tiny bit.

A silence formed between them but she wasn't feeling very comfortable in it. The cistern was seven feet deep and, thankfully, she'd used up the top two feet of it in her first two months here. Thankfully, they were both tall enough to stand in the five feet of water still remaining, rather than Tyler having to tread water with a broken ankle. It was also just four feet square so they were jostling and bumping underneath the water despite having their backs pressed against opposite sides.

The water was cool, without being cold. At least not at first. It was starting to chill her and she could feel the panic approaching and...

"Talk to me, please!" She begged before she went off the deep end. The fire's roar beyond their shelter blanket and the steel lid over the cistern was muted, but growing fast.

"Right, my apologies, ma'am," his tone which had thinned a little under the pain had shifted back to more solid. "I was just a bit perplexed is all. By our current situation. It's awkward to be bumping hips and, uh, other things with a beautiful woman under such circumstances."

"Which are?"

"Ms. Swallow Hill, I don't even know your name."

Before she could answer, he hurried on.

"But your voice, you could make a man die happy just to hear such a thing over his grave. So sure and confident and female. It's an amazing thing, I'm telling you. And then when I finally saw you," he let out a low whistle. Not a wolf whistle, but rather one of deep appreciation. "I didn't know anyone built women who looked like you. One who stood as tall and straight as a ballerina but shaped like a goddess."

"Huh!" She tried to pull herself together. She really did. It wasn't working. "That can't be."

"But it's truth."

"But it can't," and she felt about as naïve as a swallow first leaving its nest.

"Tell me why?"

"Because…" She didn't even know why. "Because—" she tried again with no more success, having to raise her voice as the fire's roar built. "Because I'm no more ballerina than goddess. I guess the confident part is right…maybe. It must be, because it pushes men away like mad." And he saw the dancer in her? She could still feel that deep inside, but no man had ever said such a thing to her.

"Then you have been—and please don't take this wrong, Ms. Swallow Hill—spending your time with a bunch of fools."

She reached out in the dark, lost for a moment in the disorienting darkness, and tentatively brushed a hand down his chest. It felt safe and right, huddled together in here as the fire burned toward them. She suppressed a shiver against the cool water.

"Living in my glass tower, can't say I've been spending time with much of anyone."

"I like the sound of that even better. Less competition for me. Not so long ago I swore I was going to get to know the lady of Swallow Hill before this summer was over."

Marta could feel the heat rising to her own face and was glad for the darkness. "I, uh, might have made a similar swear about this certain deep-voiced pilot I know." Which she couldn't believe she'd just admitted. "Say something else. Anything else."

"Well…" he tried to keep his tone light despite the tension she could feel where her hand still rested against his chest. A good man to have around in a bad situation. "The skinny dipping wasn't a completely idle suggestion. I have a pal with a big ranch down in Texas. Horse ranch. Do you ride?"

"Willing to learn," she didn't let loose the bubble of a laugh building in her throat for fear that it would emerge as a babble of panic instead.

"Some fine places there to take a lady," Tyler continued resting a hand over hers, "if she's of a mind. Fine places. Not another soul for miles in any direction."

"I might be open to that," Marta slapped her free hand over her mouth. "I can't believe I just said that." The heat flashed back into her cheeks.

Then her face kept heating.

And heating.

Their breathing air was—

"Okay, Swallow Hill. You listen close," Tyler's smooth and calm disappeared and he started speaking quickly. Dead serious now. "It's going to get hot in here, unbearably hot. And then it will get hotter. You hold down the corners of the fire blanket, keep its edges under the water. I'll do the same with my end. You're going to want to rip off the blanket. Don't! Our lives may depend on that."

Marta ducked her face down into the cool water, which only made the air feel twice as hot when she surfaced. She reached around Tyler, grabbed one end of the foil fire shelter and held it firmly behind him under the water. He did the same behind her. They were embracing…to save their lives. *Don't get stupid, Marta!*

"It all depends," Tyler continued, now talking hurriedly, "how fast the concrete and the water heat up. But do not pull the blanket aside until I tell you. No matter what. Do you understand? Do you…"

She nodded, which was pointless in the dark. They were going to be boiled alive. But she couldn't speak.

The concrete wall she was leaning against was no longer cold, it was comfortably warm. She shifted away from the wall, the warmth was creepy, felt dangerous.

Bumped into Tyler, chest to chest, but there was nowhere to go.

"Kiss me."

"What?" She had to shout to be heard over the building roar.

"I want to have kissed you *before* we survive this."

She wished she could see his face, his eyes, how he was looking at her.

The wall behind her was definitely warm now.

But she hadn't needed to see him before this moment. She heard his voice, just as she had all season; it became the center of her thoughts.

She leaned in and kissed him as the roar deafened her. She clung to him as long as she could, but she had to break apart to get air.

It was so hot.

She dragged in a breath.

The air was fire in her lungs.

"Scream!" He shouted at her. "It's okay!"

The wall behind her was now hot when she bumped it. The water was starting to warm up. She held onto Tyler. Held onto their fragile shelter where it had been pulled down behind him. The air inside the small bubble of the fire shelter inside the concrete cistern was so hot it scalded her lungs. It—

The scream that ripped from her chest was echoed by the scream from his as the fire rolled over them.

9

At some point Marta stopped screaming.

The pain had eased.

The agony of each breath.

She floated in the dark, wrapped tight around a man. Around Tyler. Her end of the foil shelter was still tight in her fists.

"Am I dead?" Then a horrible thought struck her and she gasped out, "Are you dead?"

His soft chuckle reassured her infinitely.

"Can we open the shelter yet?"

"Not yet," his voice was a whisper.

"But the fire's roar..." It was gone.

"The area around us is still too hot. Give it a few minutes. Besides…"

"Besides what?"

"I wouldn't mind kissing you *after* we survived this."

Marta decided she wouldn't mind either, not with a man who kissed as well as he did.

They only had a few moments, that she thoroughly appreciated, before the heavy pounding of an approaching helicopter sounded loud outside the cistern.

Tyler broke off the kiss, but didn't release his tight hold on her.

"That, Ms. Swallow Hill, is how we know it's cool enough to leave."

Together they pushed the blanket up against the heavy steel lid and levered it open. It dropped aside with a loud clang of steel on concrete.

They tossed the foil blanket over the hot concrete and she pulled herself up to sit on the broad rim, and then helped Tyler up to join her. He flinched when he banged his broken ankle against her, but remained stoic. A good man to have beside you…

beside her. A Black Hawk was settling onto the flat spot just below the tower. Everywhere around them was black char. The fire had burned every living thing in its path. Even now, other helicopters and a pair of tankers were battling the flames farther down the slope.

The tower!

She looked up. It still stood. The soaking Tyler gave it right before he crashed had saved it. The swallows came swooping in, complained that the box was gone, had been burned away, and then all flew off again.

"I'll bring you a new one next year," she called after them.

A silence settled as the Black Hawk's engines wound down.

"You're all red, Ms. Swallow Hill."

They only had moments before his friends arrived from the helicopter.

She was worried about facing Tyler. They had been through the heart of a fire together. They didn't know each other— but they'd said things. Shared things.

Be brave! She forced herself to look at him.

"You too." Bright red. His skin flushed brighter than a sunburn though she could see it was easing already. "Cooked like lobsters."

"Could be our first dinner date," he noted in that dry tone of his.

"Not a chance. Never had lobster and now I never will." Then she thought that, of course, she should have known—her Mama was always right. She nodded up toward the tower, "But you come visiting and I'll make the best spaghetti sauce you've ever had."

His smile was deep and proved that rugged and handsome could definitely be on the same face.

"Tell me one thing, Ms. Hill."

Her courteous, deeply-voiced Coloradan was back. With his easy humor and very good face. A man she wouldn't mind getting to know much, much better.

What secrets could she keep from such a man?

Tell him one thing?

"Anything," and she knew it was a promise.

"What's your name, Ms. Swallow Hill?"

"I offer you 'anything,' and that's the best you've got?"

She tried to shove him back into the tank, but he caught her up in his arms and gave her one of those deep, desperate kisses. Just like when they'd been at death's door, except now he was just doing it because he wanted to.

Because she wanted him to.

About the Author

M. L. Buchman has over 40 novels in print. His military romantic suspense books have been named Barnes & Noble and NPR "Top 5 of the year" and Booklist "Top 10 of the Year." In addition to romance, he also writes thrillers, fantasy, and science fiction.

In among his career as a corporate project manager he has: rebuilt and single-handed a fifty-foot sailboat, both flown and jumped out of airplanes, designed and built two houses, and bicycled solo around the world. He is now making his living as a full-time writer on the Oregon Coast with his beloved wife. He is constantly amazed at what you can do with a degree in Geophysics. You may keep up with his writing by subscribing to his newsletter at

www.mlbuchman.com.

Wildfire at Dawn
(a Firehawks "Smokejumpers
Trilogy" romance excerpt)

Mount Hood Aviation's lead smokejumper
Johnny Akbar Jepps rolled out of his lower
bunk careful not to bang his head on the
upper. Well, he tried to roll out, but every
muscle fought him, making it more a crawl
than a roll.

He checked the clock on his phone. Late morning.

He'd slept twenty of the last twenty-four hours and his body felt as if he'd spent the entire time in one position. The coarse plank flooring had been worn smooth by thousands of feet hitting exactly this same spot year in and year out for decades. He managed to stand upright…then he felt it, his shoulders and legs screamed.

Oh, right.

The New Tillamook Burn. Just about the nastiest damn blaze he'd fought in a decade of jumping wildfires. Two hundred thousand acres—over three hundred square miles—of rugged Pacific Coast Range forest, poof! The worst forest fire in a decade for the Pacific Northwest, but they'd killed it off without a single fatality or losing a single town. There'd been a few bigger ones, out in the flatter eastern part of Oregon state. But that much area— mostly on terrain too steep to climb even when it wasn't on fire—had been a horror.

Akbar opened the blackout curtain and winced against the summer brightness of blue sky and towering trees that lined the firefighter's camp. Tim was gone from the upper bunk, without kicking Akbar on his way out. He must have been as hazed out as Akbar felt.

He did a couple of side stretches and could feel every single minute of the eight straight days on the wildfire to contain the bastard, then the excruciating nine days more to convince it that it was dead enough to hand off to a Type II incident mop-up crew. Not since his beginning days on a hotshot crew had he spent seventeen days on a single fire.

And in all that time nothing more than catnaps in the acrid safety of the "black"— the burned-over section of a fire, black with char and stark with no hint of green foliage. The mop-up crews would be out there for weeks before it was dead past restarting, but at least it was truly done in. That fire wasn't merely contained; they'd killed it bad.

Yesterday morning, after demobilizing, his team of smokies had pitched into their bunks. No wonder he was so damned sore.

His stretches worked out the worst of the kinks but he still must be looking like an old man stumbling about.

He looked down at the sheets. Damn it. They'd been fresh before he went to the fire, now he'd have to wash them again. He'd been too exhausted to shower before sleeping and they were all smeared with the dirt and soot that he could still feel caking his skin. Two-Tall Tim, his number two man and as tall as two of Akbar, kinda, wasn't in his bunk. His towel was missing from the hook.

Shower. Shower would be good. He grabbed his own towel and headed down the dark, narrow hall to the far end of the bunk house. Every one of the dozen doors of his smoke teams were still closed, smokies still sacked out. A glance down another corridor and he could see that at least a couple of the Mount Hood Aviation helicopter crews were up, but most still had closed doors with no hint of light from open curtains sliding under them. All of MHA had gone above and beyond on this one.

"Hey, Tim." Sure enough, the tall Eurasian was in one of the shower stalls, propped up against the back wall letting the hot water stream over him.

"Akbar the Great lives," Two-Tall sounded half asleep.

"Mostly. Doghouse?" Akbar stripped down and hit the next stall. The old plywood dividers were flimsy with age and gray with too many showers. The Mount Hood Aviation firefighters' Hoodie One base camp had been a kids' summer camp for decades. Long since defunct, MHA had taken it over and converted the playfields into landing areas for their helicopters, and regraded the main road into a decent airstrip for the spotter and jump planes.

"Doghouse? Hell, yeah. I'm like ten thousand calories short." Two-Tall found some energy in his voice at the idea of a trip into town.

The Doghouse Inn was in the nearest town. Hood River lay about a half hour down the mountain and had exactly what they needed: smokejumper-sized portions and a very high ratio of awesomely fit young women come to windsurf the Columbia Gorge. The Gorge, which formed the Washington and Oregon border, provided a fantastically target-rich environment for a smokejumper too long in the woods.

"You're too tall to be short of anything," Akbar knew he was being a little slow to reply, but he'd only been awake for minutes.

"You're like a hundred thousand calories short of being even a halfway decent size," Tim was obviously recovering faster than he was.

"Just because my parents loved me instead of tying me to a rack every night ain't my problem, buddy."

He scrubbed and soaped and scrubbed some more until he felt mostly clean.

"I'm telling you, Two-Tall. Whoever invented the hot shower, that's the dude we should give the Nobel prize to."

"You say that every time."

"You arguing?"

He heard Tim give a satisfied groan as some muscle finally let go under the steamy hot water. "Not for a second."

Akbar stepped out and walked over to the line of sinks, smearing a hand back and forth to wipe the condensation from the sheet of stainless steel screwed to the wall. His hazy reflection still sported several smears of char.

"You so purdy, Akbar."

"Purdier than you, Two-Tall." He headed back into the shower to get the last of it.

"So not. You're jealous."

Akbar wasn't the least bit jealous. Yes, despite his lean height, Tim was handsome enough to sweep up any ladies he wanted.

But on his own, Akbar did pretty damn well himself. What he didn't have in height, he made up for with a proper smokejumper's muscled build. Mixed with his tan-dark Indian complexion, he did fine.

The real fun, of course, was when the two of them went cruising together. The women never knew what to make of the two of them side by side. The contrast kept them off balance enough to open even more doors.

He smiled as he toweled down. It also didn't hurt that their opening answer to "what do you do" was "I jump out of planes to fight forest fires."

Worked every damn time. God he loved this job.

# # #

The small town of Hood River, a winding half-an-hour down the mountain from the MHA base camp, was hopping. Mid-June, colleges letting out. Students and the younger set of professors high-tailing it to the Gorge. They packed the bars and breweries and sidewalk cafes. Suddenly every other car on the street had a wind-surfing board tied on the roof.

The snooty rich folks were up at the historic Timberline Lodge on Mount Hood itself, not far in the other direction from MHA. Down here it was a younger, thrill seeker set and you could feel the energy.

There were other restaurants in town that might have better pickings, but the Doghouse Inn was MHA tradition and it was a good luck charm—no smokie in his right mind messed with that. This was the bar where all of the MHA crew hung out.

It didn't look like much from the outside, just a worn old brick building beaten by the Gorge's violent weather. Aged before its time, which had been long ago.

But inside was awesome. A long wooden bar stretched down one side with a half-jillion microbrew taps and a small but well-stocked kitchen at the far end. The dark wood paneling, even on the ceiling, was barely visible beneath thousands of pictures of doghouses sent from patrons all over the world. Miniature dachshunds in ornately decorated shoeboxes, massive Newfoundlands in backyard mansions that could easily house hundreds of their smaller kin, and everything in between. A gigantic Snoopy atop his doghouse in full Red Baron fighting gear dominated the far wall. Rumor said Shulz himself had been here two owners before and drawn it.

Tables were grouped close together, some for standing and drinking, others for sitting and eating.

"Amy, sweetheart!" Two-Tall called out as they entered the bar. The perky redhead came out from behind the bar to receive a hug from Tim. Akbar got one in turn, so he wasn't complaining. Cute as could be and about his height; her hugs were better than taking most women to bed. Of course, Gerald the cook and the bar's co-owner was big enough and strong enough to squish either Tim or Akbar if they got even a tiny step out of line with his wife. Gerald was one amazingly lucky man.

Akbar grabbed a Walking Man stout and turned to assess the crowd. A couple of the air jocks were in. Carly and Steve were at a little table for two in the corner, obviously not interested in anyone's company but each others. Damn, that had happened fast. New guy on the base swept up one of the most beautiful women on the planet. One of these days he'd have to ask Steve how he'd done that. Or maybe not. It looked like they were settling in for the long haul; the big "M" was so not his own first choice.

Carly was also one of the best FBANs in the business. Akbar was a good Fire Behavior Analyst, had to be or he wouldn't have made it to first stick—lead smokie of the whole MHA crew. But Carly was something else again. He'd always found the Flame Witch, as she was often called, daunting and a bit scary besides; she knew the fire better than it did itself. Steve had latched on to one seriously driven lady. More power to him.

The selection of female tourists was especially good today, but no other smokies in yet. They'd be in soon enough…most of them had groaned awake and said they were coming as he and Two-Tall kicked their hallway doors, but not until they'd been on their way out—he and Tim had first pick. Actually some of the smokies were coming, others had told them quite succinctly where they could go—but hey, jumping into fiery hell is what they did for a living anyway, so no big change there.

A couple of the chopper pilots had nailed down a big table right in the middle of the bustling seating area: Jeannie, Mickey, and Vern. Good "field of fire" in the immediate area.

He and Tim headed over, but Akbar managed to snag the chair closest to the really hot lady with down-her-back curling dark-auburn hair at the next table over—set just right to see her profile easily. Hard shot, sitting there with her parents, but damn she was amazing. And if that was her mom, it said the woman would be good looking for a long time to come.

Two-Tall grimaced at him and Akbar offered him a comfortable "beat out your ass" grin. But this one didn't feel like that. Maybe it was the whole parental thing. He sat back and kept his mouth shut.

He made sure that Two-Tall could see his interest. That made Tim honor bound to try and cut Akbar out of the running.

# # #

Laura Jenson had spotted them coming into the restaurant. Her dad was only moments behind.

"Those two are walking like they just climbed off their first-ever horseback ride."

She had to laugh, they did. So stiff and awkward they barely managed to move upright. They didn't look like first-time wind-surfers, aching from the unexpected workout. They'd also walked in like they thought they were two gifts to god, which was even funnier. She turned away to avoid laughing in their faces. Guys who thought like that rarely appreciated getting a reality check.

A couple minutes later, at a nod from her dad, she did a careful sideways glance. Sure enough, they'd joined in with a group of friends who were seated at the next table behind her. The short one, shorter than she was by four or five inches, sat to one side. He was doing the old stare without staring routine, as if she were so naïve as to not recognize it. His ridiculously tall companion sat around the next turn of the table to her other side.

Then the tall one raised his voice enough to be heard easily over her dad's story about the latest goings-on at the local drone manufacturer. His company was the first one to be certified by the FAA for limited testing on wildfire and search-and-rescue overflights. She wanted to hear about it, but the tall guy had a deep voice that carried as if he were barrel-chested rather than pencil thin.

"Hell of fire, wasn't it? Where do you think we'll be jumping next?"

Smokies. Well, maybe they had some right to arrogance, but it didn't gain any ground with her.

"Please make it a small one," a woman who Laura couldn't see right behind her chimed in. "I wouldn't mind getting to sleep at least a couple times this summer if I'm gonna be flying you guys around."

Laura tried to listen to her dad, but the patter behind her was picking up speed.

Another guy, "Yeah, know what you mean, Jeannie. I caught myself flying along trying to figure out how to fit crows and Stellar jays with little belly tanks to douse the flames. Maybe get a turkey vulture with a Type I heavy load classification."

"At least you weren't knocked down," Jeannie again. Laura liked her voice; she sounded fun. "Damn tree took out my rotor. They got it aloft, but maintenance hasn't signed it off for fire yet. They better have it done before the next call." A woman who knew no fear—or at least knew about getting back up on the horse.

A woman who flew choppers; that was kind of cool actually. Laura had thought about smokejumping, but not very hard. She enjoyed being down in the forest too much. She'd been born and bred to be a guide. And her job at Timberline Lodge let her do a lot of that.

Dad was working on the search-and-rescue testing. Said they could find a human body heat signature, even in deep trees.

"Hey," Laura finally managed to drag her attention wholly back to her parents. "If you guys need somewhere to test them, I'd love to play. As the Lodge's activities director, I'm down rivers, out on lakes, and leading mountain hikes on most days. All with tourists. And you know how much trouble they get into."

Mom laughed, she knew exactly what her daughter meant. Laura had come by the trade right down the matrilineal line. Grandma had been a fishing and hunting tour guide out of Nome, Alaska back when a woman had to go to Alaska to do more than be a teacher or nurse. Mom had done the same until she met a man from the lower forty-eight who promised they could ride horses almost year-round in Oregon. Laura had practically grown up on horseback, leading group rides deep into the Oregon Wilderness first with her mom and, by the time she was in her mid-teens, on her own.

They chatted about the newest drone technology for a while.

The guy with the big, deep voice finally faded away, one less guy to worry about hitting on her. But out of her peripheral vision, she could still see the other guy, the short one with the tan-dark skin, tight curly black hair, and shoulders like Atlas.

He'd teased the tall guy as they sat down and then gone silent. Not quite watching her; the same way she was not quite watching him.

Her dad missed what was going on, but her mom's smile was definitely giving her shit about it.

Available at fine retailers everywhere

More information at:
www.mlbuchman.com

Other works by M.L. Buchman

Firehawks (romantic suspense)

Pure Heat
Wildfire at Dawn
Full Blaze
Wildfire at Larch Creek
Wildfire on the Skagit
Hot Point

The Night Stalkers (romantic suspense)

The Night Is Mine
I Own the Dawn
Daniel's Christmas
Wait Until Dark
Frank's Independence Day
Peter's Christmas
Take Over at Midnight
Light Up the Night
Bring On the Dusk
Target of the Heart

Angelo's Hearth (romance)

Where Dreams are Born
Where Dreams Reside
Maria's Christmas Table
Where Dreams Unfold
Where Dreams Are Written

Dead Chef (thriller)

Swap Out!

One Chef!

Two Chef!

Dieties Anonymous (fantasy)

Cookbook from Hell: Reheated

Saviors 101

Other SF/F Titles

Nara

Monk's Maze

www.ingramcontent.com/pod-product-compliance
Lightning Source LLC
Chambersburg PA
CBHW050500110726
47899CB00003B/1013